SELECTED POEMS
1965–1975

by the same author

DEATH OF A NATURALIST

DOOR INTO THE DARK

WINTERING OUT

NORTH

FIELD WORK

STATION ISLAND

SWEENEY ASTRAY

SEAMUS HEANEY

Selected Poems 1965-1975

faber and faber
LONDON · BOSTON

First published in 1980
by Faber and Faber Limited
3 Queen Square London WC1N 3AU
Reprinted 1981, 1983 and 1985
Printed in Great Britain by
Richard Clay (The Chaucer Press) Ltd,
Bungay, Suffolk
All rights reserved

British Library Cataloguing in Publication Data
Heaney, Seamus
Selected poems, 1965–1975.
821'.9'14   PR6058. E2

ISBN 0–571–11644–2
ISBN 0–571–11617–5 Pbk

For Marie
and Michael and Christopher
and Catherine Ann

Contents

from
Death of a Naturalist

DIGGING

Between my finger and my thumb
The squat pen rests; snug as a gun.

Under my window, a clean rasping sound
When the spade sinks into gravelly ground:
My father, digging. I look down

Till his straining rump among the flowerbeds
Bends low, comes up twenty years away
Stooping in rhythm through potato drills
Where he was digging.

The coarse boot nestled on the lug, the shaft
Against the inside knee was levered firmly.
He rooted out tall tops, buried the bright edge deep
To scatter new potatoes that we picked
Loving their cool hardness in our hands.

By God, the old man could handle a spade.
Just like his old man.

My grandfather cut more turf in a day
Than any other man on Toner's bog.
Once I carried him milk in a bottle
Corked sloppily with paper. He straightened up
To drink it, then fell to right away

Nicking and slicing neatly, heaving sods
Over his shoulder, going down and down
For the good turf. Digging.

The cold smell of potato mould, the squelch and slap
Of soggy peat, the curt cuts of an edge
Through living roots awaken in my head.
But I've no spade to follow men like them.

Between my finger and my thumb
The squat pen rests.
I'll dig with it.

DEATH OF A NATURALIST

All year the flax-dam festered in the heart
Of the townland; green and heavy headed
Flax had rotted there, weighted down by huge sods.
Daily it sweltered in the punishing sun.
Bubbles gargled delicately, bluebottles
Wove a strong gauze of sound around the smell.
There were dragon-flies, spotted butterflies,
But best of all was the warm thick slobber
Of frogspawn that grew like clotted water
In the shade of the banks. Here, every spring
I would fill jampotfuls of the jellied
Specks to range on window-sills at home,
On shelves at school, and wait and watch until
The fattening dots burst into nimble-
Swimming tadpoles. Miss Walls would tell us how
The daddy frog was called a bullfrog
And how he croaked and how the mammy frog
Laid hundreds of little eggs and this was
Frogspawn. You could tell the weather by frogs too
For they were yellow in the sun and brown
In rain.

　　Then one hot day when fields were rank
With cowdung in the grass the angry frogs
Invaded the flax-dam; I ducked through hedges
To a coarse croaking that I had not heard

Before. The air was thick with a bass chorus.
Right down the dam gross-bellied frogs were cocked
On sods; their loose necks pulsed like sails. Some hopped:
The slap and plop were obscene threats. Some sat
Poised like mud grenades, their blunt heads farting.
I sickened, turned, and ran. The great slime kings
Were gathered there for vengeance and I knew
That if I dipped my hand the spawn would clutch it.

THE BARN

Threshed corn lay piled like grit of ivory
Or solid as cement in two-lugged sacks.
The musty dark hoarded an armoury
Of farmyard implements, harness, plough-socks.

The floor was mouse-grey, smooth, chilly concrete.
There were no windows, just two narrow shafts
Of gilded motes, crossing, from air-holes slit
High in each gable. The one door meant no draughts

All summer when the zinc burned like an oven.
A scythe's edge, a clean spade, a pitch-fork's prongs:
Slowly bright objects formed when you went in.
Then you felt cobwebs clogging up your lungs

And scuttled fast into the sunlit yard.
And into nights when bats were on the wing
Over the rafters of sleep, where bright eyes stared
From piles of grain in corners, fierce, unblinking.

The dark gulfed like a roof-space. I was chaff
To be pecked up when birds shot through the air-slits.
I lay face-down to shun the fear above.
The two-lugged sacks moved in like great blind rats.

BLACKBERRY-PICKING

For Philip Hobsbaum

Late August, given heavy rain and sun
For a full week, the blackberries would ripen.
At first, just one, a glossy purple clot
Among others, red, green, hard as a knot.
You ate that first one and its flesh was sweet
Like thickened wine: summer's blood was in it
Leaving stains upon the tongue and lust for
Picking. Then red ones inked up and that hunger
Sent us out with milk-cans, pea-tins, jam-pots
Where briars scratched and wet grass bleached our boots.
Round hayfields, cornfields and potato-drills
We trekked and picked until the cans were full,
Until the tinkling bottom had been covered
With green ones, and on top big dark blobs burned
Like a plate of eyes. Our hands were peppered
With thorn pricks, our palms sticky as Bluebeard's.

We hoarded the fresh berries in the byre.
But when the bath was filled we found a fur,
A rat-grey fungus, glutting on our cache.
The juice was stinking too. Once off the bush
The fruit fermented, the sweet flesh would turn sour.
I always felt like crying. It wasn't fair
That all the lovely canfuls smelt of rot.
Each year I hoped they'd keep, knew they would not.

CHURNING DAY

A thick crust, coarse-grained as limestone rough-cast,
hardened gradually on top of the four crocks
that stood, large pottery bombs, in the small pantry.
After the hot brewery of gland, cud and udder
cool porous earthenware fermented the buttermilk
for churning day, when the hooped churn was scoured
with plumping kettles and the busy scrubber
echoed daintily on the seasoned wood.
It stood then, purified, on the flagged kitchen floor.

Out came the four crocks, spilled their heavy lip
of cream, their white insides, into the sterile churn.
The staff, like a great whisky muddler fashioned
in deal wood, was plunged in, the lid fitted.
My mother took first turn, set up rhythms
that slugged and thumped for hours. Arms ached.
Hands blistered. Cheeks and clothes were spattered
with flabby milk.

                    Where finally gold flecks
began to dance. They poured hot water then,
sterilized a birchwood-bowl
and little corrugated butter-spades.
Their short stroke quickened, suddenly
a yellow curd was weighting the churned up white,

heavy and rich, coagulated sunlight
that they fished, dripping, in a wide tin strainer,
heaped up like gilded gravel in the bowl.

The house would stink long after churning day,
acrid as a sulphur mine. The empty crocks
were ranged along the wall again, the butter
in soft printed slabs was piled on pantry shelves.
And in the house we moved with gravid ease,
our brains turned crystals full of clean deal churns,
the plash and gurgle of the sour-breathed milk,
the pat and slap of small spades on wet lumps.

FOLLOWER

My father worked with a horse-plough,
His shoulders globed like a full sail strung
Between the shafts and the furrow.
The horses strained at his clicking tongue.

An expert. He would set the wing
And fit the bright steel-pointed sock.
The sod rolled over without breaking.
At the headrig, with a single pluck

Of reins, the sweating team turned round
And back into the land. His eye
Narrowed and angled at the ground,
Mapping the furrow exactly.

I stumbled in his hob-nailed wake,
Fell sometimes on the polished sod;
Sometimes he rode me on his back
Dipping and rising to his plod.

I wanted to grow up and plough,
To close one eye, stiffen my arm.
All I ever did was follow
In his broad shadow round the farm.

I was a nuisance, tripping, falling,
Yapping always. But today
It is my father who keeps stumbling
Behind me, and will not go away.

MID-TERM BREAK

I sat all morning in the college sick bay
Counting bells knelling classes to a close.
At two o'clock our neighbours drove me home.

In the porch I met my father crying—
He had always taken funerals in his stride—
And Big Jim Evans saying it was a hard blow.

The baby cooed and laughed and rocked the pram
When I came in, and I was embarrassed
By old men standing up to shake my hand

And tell me they were 'sorry for my trouble';
Whispers informed strangers I was the eldest,
Away at school, as my mother held my hand

In hers and coughed out angry tearless sighs.
At ten o'clock the ambulance arrived
With the corpse, stanched and bandaged by the nurses.

Next morning I went up into the room. Snowdrops
And candles soothed the bedside; I saw him
For the first time in six weeks. Paler now,

Wearing a poppy bruise on his left temple,
He lay in the four foot box as in his cot.
No gaudy scars, the bumper knocked him clear.

A four foot box, a foot for every year.

AT A POTATO DIGGING

A mechanical digger wrecks the drill,
Spins up a dark shower of roots and mould.
Labourers swarm in behind, stoop to fill
Wicker creels. Fingers go dead in the cold.

Like crows attacking crow-black fields, they stretch
A higgledy line from hedge to headland;
Some pairs keep breaking ragged ranks to fetch
A full creel to the pit and straighten, stand

Tall for a moment but soon stumble back
To fish a new load from the crumbled surf.
Heads bow, trunks bend, hands fumble towards the black
Mother. Processional stooping through the turf

Recurs mindlessly as autumn. Centuries
Of fear and homage to the famine god
Toughen the muscles behind their humbled knees,
Make a seasonal altar of the sod.

II

Flint-white, purple. They lie scattered
like inflated pebbles. Native
to the black hutch of clay
where the halved seed shot and clotted

these knobbed and slit-eyed tubers seem
the petrified hearts of drills. Split
by the spade, they show white as cream.

Good smells exude from crumbled earth.
The rough bark of humus erupts
knots of potatoes (a clean birth)
whose solid feel, whose wet inside
promises taste of ground and root.
To be piled in pits; live skulls, blind-eyed.

III

Live skulls, blind-eyed, balanced on
wild higgledy skeletons
scoured the land in 'forty-five,
wolfed the blighted root and died.

The new potato, sound as stone,
putrefied when it had lain
three days in the long clay pit.
Millions rotted along with it.

Mouths tightened in, eyes died hard,
faces chilled to a plucked bird.
In a million wicker huts
beaks of famine snipped at guts.

A people hungering from birth,
grubbing, like plants, in the bitch earth,
were grafted with a great sorrow.
Hope rotted like a marrow.

Stinking potatoes fouled the land,
pits turned pus into filthy mounds:

and where potato diggers are
you still smell the running sore.

Under a gay flotilla of gulls
The rhythm deadens, the workers stop.
Brown bread and tea in bright canfuls
Are served for lunch. Dead-beat, they flop

Down in the ditch and take their fill,
Thankfully breaking timeless fasts;
Then, stretched on the faithless ground, spill
Libations of cold tea, scatter crusts.

THE DIVINER

Cut from the green hedge a forked hazel stick
That he held tight by the arms of the V:
Circling the terrain, hunting the pluck
Of water, nervous, but professionally

Unfussed. The pluck came sharp as a sting.
The rod jerked down with precise convulsions,
Spring water suddenly broadcasting
Through a green aerial its secret stations.

The bystanders would ask to have a try.
He handed them the rod without a word.
It lay dead in their grasp till nonchalantly
He gripped expectant wrists. The hazel stirred.

LOVERS ON ARAN

The timeless waves, bright sifting, broken glass,
Came dazzling around, into the rocks,
Came glinting, sifting from the Americas

To possess Aran. Or did Aran rush
To throw wide arms of rock around a tide
That yielded with an ebb, with a soft crash?

Did sea define the land or land the sea?
Each drew new meaning from the waves' collision.
Sea broke on land to full identity.

POEM

For Marie

Love, I shall perfect for you the child
Who diligently potters in my brain
Digging with heavy spade till sods were piled
Or puddling through muck in a deep drain.

Yearly I would sow my yard-long garden.
I'd strip a layer of sods to build the wall
That was to exclude sow and pecking hen.
Yearly, admitting these, the sods would fall.

Or in the sucking clabber I would splash
Delightedly and dam the flowing drain
But always my bastions of clay and mush
Would burst before the rising autumn rain.

Love, you shall perfect for me this child
Whose small imperfect limits would keep breaking:
Within new limits now, arrange the world
Within our walls, within our golden ring.

PERSONAL HELICON

For Michael Longley

As a child, they could not keep me from wells
And old pumps with buckets and windlasses.
I loved the dark drop, the trapped sky, the smells
Of waterweed, fungus and dank moss.

One, in a brickyard, with a rotted board top.
I savoured the rich crash when a bucket
Plummeted down at the end of a rope.
So deep you saw no reflection in it.

A shallow one under a dry stone ditch
Fructified like any aquarium.
When you dragged out long roots from the soft mulch
A white face hovered over the bottom.

Others had echoes, gave back your own call
With a clean new music in it. And one
Was scaresome for there, out of ferns and tall
Foxgloves, a rat slapped across my reflection.

Now, to pry into roots, to finger slime,
To stare, big-eyed Narcissus, into some spring
Is beneath all adult dignity. I rhyme
To see myself, to set the darkness echoing.

from
Door into the Dark

THE FORGE

All I know is a door into the dark.
Outside, old axles and iron hoops rusting;
Inside, the hammered anvil's short-pitched ring,
The unpredictable fantail of sparks
Or hiss when a new shoe toughens in water.
The anvil must be somewhere in the centre,
Horned as a unicorn, at one end square,
Set there immoveable: an altar
Where he expends himself in shape and music.
Sometimes, leather-aproned, hairs in his nose,
He leans out on the jamb, recalls a clatter
Of hoofs where traffic is flashing in rows;
Then grunts and goes in, with a slam and flick
To beat real iron out, to work the bellows.

THATCHER

Bespoke for weeks, he turned up some morning
Unexpectedly, his bicycle slung
With a light ladder and a bag of knives.
He eyed the old rigging, poked at the eaves,

Opened and handled sheaves of lashed wheat-straw.
Next, the bundled rods: hazel and willow
Were flicked for weight, twisted in case they'd snap.
It seemed he spent the morning warming up:

Then fixed the ladder, laid out well honed blades
And snipped at straw and sharpened ends of rods
That, bent in two, made a white-pronged staple
For pinning down his world, handful by handful.

Couchant for days on sods above the rafters
He shaved and flushed the butts, stitched all together
Into a sloped honeycomb, a stubble patch,
And left them gaping at his Midas touch.

THE PENINSULA

When you have nothing more to say, just drive
For a day all round the peninsula.
The sky is tall as over a runway,
The land without marks so you will not arrive

But pass through, though always skirting landfall.
At dusk, horizons drink down sea and hill,
The ploughed field swallows the whitewashed gable
And you're in the dark again. Now recall

The glazed foreshore and silhouetted log,
That rock where breakers shredded into rags,
The leggy birds stilted on their own legs,
Islands riding themselves out into the fog

And drive back home, still with nothing to say
Except that now you will uncode all landscapes
By this: things founded clean on their own shapes,
Water and ground in their extremity.

REQUIEM FOR THE CROPPIES

The pockets of our great coats full of barley—
No kitchens on the run, no striking camp—
We moved quick and sudden in our own country.
The priest lay behind ditches with the tramp.
A people, hardly marching—on the hike—
We found new tactics happening each day:
We'd cut through reins and rider with the pike
And stampede cattle into infantry,
Then retreat through hedges where cavalry must be
    thrown.
Until, on Vinegar Hill, the fatal conclave.
Terraced thousands died, shaking scythes at cannon.
The hillside blushed, soaked in our broken wave.
They buried us without shroud or coffin
And in August the barley grew up out of the grave.

UNDINE

He slashed the briars, shovelled up grey silt
To give me right of way in my own drains
And I ran quick for him, cleaned out my rust.

He halted, saw me finally disrobed,
Running clear, with apparent unconcern.
Then he walked by me. I rippled and I churned

Where ditches intersected near the river
Until he dug a spade deep in my flank
And took me to him. I swallowed his trench

Gratefully, dispersing myself for love
Down in his roots, climbing his brassy grain—
But once he knew my welcome, I alone

Could give him subtle increase and reflection.
He explored me so completely, each limb
Lost its cold freedom. Human, warmed to him.

THE WIFE'S TALE

When I had spread it all on linen cloth
Under the hedge, I called them over.
The hum and gulp of the thresher ran down
And the big belt slewed to a standstill, straw
Hanging undelivered in the jaws.
There was such quiet that I heard their boots
Crunching the stubble twenty yards away.

He lay down and said 'Give these fellows theirs.
I'm in no hurry,' plucking grass in handfuls
And tossing it in the air. 'That looks well.'
(He nodded at my white cloth on the grass.)
'I declare a woman could lay out a field
Though boys like us have little call for cloths.'
He winked, then watched me as I poured a cup
And buttered the thick slices that he likes.
'It's threshing better than I thought, and mind
It's good clean seed. Away over there and look.'
Always this inspection has to be made
Even when I don't know what to look for.

But I ran my hand in the half-filled bags
Hooked to the slots. It was hard as shot,
Innumerable and cool. The bags gaped
Where the chutes ran back to the stilled drum
And forks were stuck at angles in the ground

As javelins might mark lost battlefields.
I moved between them back across the stubble.

They lay in the ring of their own crusts and dregs
Smoking and saying nothing. 'There's good yield,
Isn't there?'—as proud as if he were the land itself—
'Enough for crushing and for sowing both.'
And that was it. I'd come and he had shown me
So I belonged no further to the work.
I gathered cups and folded up the cloth
And went. But they still kept their ease
Spread out, unbuttoned, grateful, under the trees.

NIGHT DRIVE

The smells of ordinariness
Were new on the night drive through France:
Rain and hay and woods on the air
Made warm draughts in the open car.

Signposts whitened relentlessly.
Montreuil, Abbéville, Beauvais
Were promised, promised, came and went,
Each place granting its name's fulfilment.

A combine groaning its way late
Bled seeds across it work-light.
A forest fire smouldered out.
One by one small cafés shut.

I thought of you continuously
A thousand miles south where Italy
Laid its loin to France on the darkened sphere.
Your ordinariness was renewed there.

AT ARDBOE POINT

Right along the lough shore
A smoke of flies
Drifts thick in the sunset.

They come smattering daintily
Against the windscreen,
The grill and bonnet whisper

At their million collisions:
It is to drive through
A hail of fine chaff.

Yet we leave no clear wake
For they open and close on us
As the air opens and closes.

To-night when we put out our light
To kiss between sheets
Their just audible siren will go

Outside the window,
Their invisible veil
Weakening the moonlight still further

And the walls will carry a rash
Of them, a green pollen.
They'll have infiltrated our clothes by morning.

If you put one under a lens
You'd be looking at a pumping body
With such outsize beaters for wings

That this visitation would seem
More drastic than Pharaoh's—
I'm told they're mosquitoes

But I'd need forests and swamps
To believe it
For these are our innocent, shuttling

Choirs, dying through
Their own live empyrean, troublesome only
As the last veil on a dancer.

A LOUGH NEAGH SEQUENCE

for the fishermen

1. UP THE SHORE

I

The lough will claim a victim every year.
It has virtue that hardens wood to stone.
There is a town sunk beneath its water.
It is the scar left by the Isle of Man.

II

At Toomebridge where it sluices towards the sea
They've set new gates and tanks against the flow.
From time to time they break the eels' journey
And lift five hundred stone in one go.

III

But up the shore in Antrim and Tyrone
There is a sense of fair play in the game.
The fishermen confront them one by one
And sail miles out, and never learn to swim.

IV

'We'll be the quicker going down', they say—
And when you argue there are no storms here,
That one hour floating's sure to land them safely—
'The lough will claim a victim every year.'

A gland agitating
mud two hundred miles in-
land, a scale of water
on water working up
estuaries, he drifted
into motion half-way
across the Atlantic,
sure as the satellite's
insinuating pull
in the ocean, as true
to his orbit.
                    Against
ebb, current, rock, rapids
a muscled icicle
that melts itself longer
and fatter, he buries
his arrival beyond
light and tidal water,
investing silt and sand
with a sleek root. By day
only the drainmaker's
spade or the mud paddler
can make him abort. Dark
delivers him hungering
down each undulation.

3. BAIT

Lamps dawdle in the field at midnight.
Three men follow their nose in the grass,
The lamps' beam their prow and compass.

The bucket's handle better not clatter now:
Silence and curious light gather bait.
Nab him, but wait

For the first shrinking, tacky on the thumb.
Let him re-settle backwards in his tunnel.
Then draw steady and he'll come.

Among the millions whorling their mud coronas
Under dewlapped leaf and bowed blades
A few are bound to be rustled in these night raids,

Innocent ventilators of the ground
Making the globe a perfect fit,
A few are bound to be cheated of it

When lamps dawdle in the field at midnight,
When fishers need a garland for the bay
And have him, where he needs to come, out of the clay.

A line goes out of sight and out of mind
Down to the soft bottom of silt and sand
Past the indifferent skill of the hunting hand.

A bouquet of small hooks coiled in the stern
Is being paid out, back to its true form,
Until the bouquet's hidden in the worm.

The boat rides forward where the line slants back.
The oars in their locks go round and round.
The eel describes his arcs without a sound.

5. LIFTING

They're busy in a high boat
That stalks towards Antrim, the power cut.
The line's a filament of smut

Drawn hand over fist
Where every three yards a hook's missed
Or taken (and the smut thickens, wrist-

Thick, a flail
Lashed into the barrel
With one swing). Each eel

Comes aboard to this welcome:
The hook left in gill or gum,
It's slapped into the barrel numb

But knits itself, four-ply,
With the furling, slippy
Haul, a knot of back and pewter belly

That stays continuously one
For each catch they fling in
Is sucked home like lubrication.

And wakes are enwound as the catch
On the morning water: which
Boat was which?

And when did this begin?
This morning, last year, when the lough first spawned?
The crews will answer, 'Once the season's in.'

6. THE RETURN

In ponds, drains, dead canals
she turns her head back,
older now, following
whim deliberately
till she's at sea in grass
and damned if she'll turn so
it's new trenches, sunk pipes,
swamps, running streams, the lough,
the river. Her stomach
shrunk, she exhilarates
in mid-water. Its throbbing
is speed through days and weeks.

Who knows now if she knows
her depth or direction;
she's passed Malin and
Tory, silent, wakeless,
a wisp, a wick that is
its own taper and light
through the weltering dark.
Where she's lost once she lays
ten thousand feet down in
her origins. The current
carries slicks of orphaned spawn.

7. VISION

Unless his hair was fine-combed
The lice, they said, would gang up
Into a mealy rope
And drag him, small, dirty, doomed

Down to the water. He was
Cautious then in riverbank
Fields. Thick as a birch trunk
That cable flexed in the grass

Every time the wind passed. Years
Later in the same fields
He stood at night when eels
Moved through the grass like hatched fears

Towards the water. To stand
In one place as the field flowed
Past, a jellied road,
To watch the eels crossing land

Re-wound his world's live girdle.
Phosphorescent, sinewed slime
Continued at his feet. Time
Confirmed the horrid cable.

THE GIVEN NOTE

On the most westerly Blasket
In a dry-stone hut
He got this air out of the night.

Strange noises were heard
By others who followed, bits of a tune
Coming in on loud weather

Though nothing like melody.
He blamed their fingers and ear
As unpractised, their fiddling easy

For he had gone alone into the island
And brought back the whole thing.
The house throbbed like his full violin.

So whether he calls it spirit music
Or not, I don't care. He took it
Out of wind off mid-Atlantic.

Still he maintains, from nowhere.
It comes off the bow gravely,
Rephrases itself into the air.

THE PLANTATION

Any point in that wood
Was a centre, birch trunks
Ghosting your bearings,
Improvising charmed rings

Wherever you stopped.
Though you walked a straight line
It might be a circle you travelled
With toadstools and stumps

Always repeating themselves.
Or did you re-pass them?
Here were blaeberries quilting the floor,
The black char of a fire

And having found them once
You were sure to find them again.
Someone had always been there
Though always you were alone.

Lovers, birdwatchers,
Campers, gipsies and tramps
Left some trace of their trades
Or their excrement.

Hedging the road so
It invited all comers
To the hush and the mush
Of its whispering treadmill,

Its limits defined,
So they thought, from outside.
They must have been thankful
For the hum of the traffic

If they ventured in
Past the picnickers' belt
Or began to recall
Tales of fog on the mountains.

You had to come back
To learn how to lose yourself,
To be pilot and stray—witch,
Hansel and Gretel in one.

SHORELINE

Turning a corner, taking a hill
In County Down, there's the sea
Sidling and settling to
The back of a hedge. Or else

A grey bottom with puddles
Dead-eyed as fish.
Haphazard tidal craters march
The corn and the grazing.

All round Antrim and westward
Two hundred miles at Moher
Basalt stands to.
Both ocean and channel

Froth at the black locks
On Ireland. And strands
Take hissing submissions
Off Wicklow and Mayo.

Take any minute. A tide
Is rummaging in
At the foot of all fields,
All cliffs and shingles.

Listen. Is it the Danes,
A black hawk bent on the sail?
Or the chinking Normans?
Or currachs hopping high

On to the sand?
Strangford, Arklow, Carrickfergus,
Belmullet and Ventry
Stay, forgotten like sentries.

BOGLAND

for T. P. Flanagan

We have no prairies
To slice a big sun at evening—
Everywhere the eye concedes to
Encroaching horizon,

Is wooed into the cyclops' eye
Of a tarn. Our unfenced country
Is bog that keeps crusting
Between the sights of the sun.

They've taken the skeleton
Of the Great Irish Elk
Out of the peat, set it up
An astounding crate full of air.

Butter sunk under
More than a hundred years
Was recovered salty and white.
The ground itself is kind, black butter

Melting and opening underfoot,
Missing its last definition
By millions of years.
They'll never dig coal here,

Only the waterlogged trunks
Of great firs, soft as pulp.
Our pioneers keep striking
Inwards and downwards,

Every layer they strip
Seems camped on before.
The bogholes might be Atlantic seepage.
The wet centre is bottomless.

from
Wintering Out

BOG OAK

A carter's trophy
split for rafters,
a cobwebbed, black,
long-seasoned rib

under the first thatch.
I might tarry
with the moustached
dead, the creel-fillers,

or eavesdrop on
their hopeless wisdom
as a blow-down of smoke
struggles over the half-door

and mizzling rain
blurs the far end
of the cart track.
The softening ruts

lead back to no
'oak groves', no
cutters of mistletoe
in the green clearings.

Perhaps I just make out
Edmund Spenser,
dreaming sunlight,
encroached upon by

geniuses who creep
'out of every corner
of the woodes and glennes'
towards watercress and carrion.

ANAHORISH

My 'place of clear water',
the first hill in the world
where springs washed into
the shiny grass

and darkened cobbles
in the bed of the lane.
Anahorish, soft gradient
of consonant, vowel-meadow,

after-image of lamps
swung through the yards
on winter evenings.
With pails and barrows

those mound-dwellers
go waist-deep in mist
to break the light ice
at wells and dunghills.

SERVANT BOY

He is wintering out
the back-end of a bad year,
swinging a hurricane-lamp
through some outhouse;

a jobber among shadows.
Old work-whore, slave-
blood, who stepped fair-hills
under each bidder's eye

and kept your patience
and your counsel, how
you draw me into
your trail. Your trail

broken from haggard to stable,
a straggle of fodder
stiffened on snow,
comes first-footing

the back doors of the little
barons: resentful
and impenitent,
carrying the warm eggs.

THE LAST MUMMER

I

Carries a stone in his pocket,
an ash-plant under his arm.

Moves out of the fog
on the lawn, pads up the terrace.

The luminous screen in the corner
has them charmed in a ring

so he stands a long time behind them.
St. George, Beelzebub and Jack Straw

can't be conjured from mist.
He catches the stick in his fist

and, shrouded, starts beating
the bars of the gate.

His boots crack the road. The stone
clatters down off the slates.

He came trammelled
in the taboos of the country

picking a nice way through
the long toils of blood

and feuding.
His tongue went whoring

among the civil tongues,
he had an eye for weather-eyes

at cross-roads and lane-ends
and could don manners

at a flutter of curtains.
His straw mask and hunch were fabulous

disappearing beyond the lamplit
slabs of a yard.

III

You dream a cricket in the hearth
and cockroach on the floor,

a line of mummers
marching out the door

as the lamp flares in the draught.
Melted snow off their feet

leaves you in peace.
Again an old year dies

on your hearthstone, for good luck.
The moon's host elevated

in a monstrance of holly trees,
he makes dark tracks, who had

untousled a first dewy path
into the summer grazing.

GIFTS OF RAIN

I

Cloudburst and steady downpour now
for days.
        Still mammal,
straw-footed on the mud,
he begins to sense weather
by his skin.

A nimble snout of flood
licks over stepping stones
and goes uprooting.
        He fords
his life by sounding.
        Soundings.

II

A man wading lost fields
breaks the pane of flood:

a flower of mud-
water blooms up to his reflection

like a cut swaying
its red spoors through a basin.

63

His hands grub
where the spade has uncastled

sunken drills, an atlantis
he depends on. So

he is hooped to where he planted
and sky and ground

are running naturally among his arms
that grope the cropping land.

III

When rains were gathering
there would be an all-night
roaring off the ford.
Their world-schooled ear

could monitor the usual
confabulations, the race
slabbering past the gable,
the Moyola harping on

its gravel beds:
all spouts by daylight
brimmed with their own airs
and overflowed each barrel

in long tresses.
I cock my ear
at an absence—
in the shared calling of blood

arrives my need
for antediluvian lore.
Soft voices of the dead
are whispering by the shore

that I would question
(and for my children's sake)
about crops rotted, river mud
glazing the baked clay floor.

IV

The tawny guttural water
spells itself: Moyola
is its own score and consort,

bedding the locale
in the utterance,
reed music, an old chanter

breathing its mists
through vowels and history.
A swollen river,

a mating call of sound
rises to pleasure me, Dives,
hoarder of common ground.

BROAGH

Riverbank, the long rigs
ending in broad docken
and a canopied pad
down to the ford.

The garden mould
bruised easily, the shower
gathering in your heelmark
was the black *O*

in *Broagh*,
its low tattoo
among the windy boortrees
and rhubarb-blades

ended almost
suddenly, like that last
gh the strangers found
difficult to manage.

ORACLE

Hide in the hollow trunk
of the willow tree,
its listening familiar,
until, as usual, they
cuckoo your name
across the fields.
You can hear them
draw the poles of stiles
as they approach
calling you out:
small mouth and ear
in a woody cleft,
lobe and larynx
of the mossy places.

TRADITIONS

For Tom Flanagan

Our guttural muse
was bulled long ago
by the alliterative tradition,
her uvula grows

vestigial, forgotten
like the coccyx
or a Brigid's Cross
yellowing in some outhouse

while custom, that 'most
sovereign mistress',
beds us down into
the British isles.

II

We are to be proud
of our Elizabethan English:
'varsity', for example,
is grass-roots stuff with us;

we 'deem' or we 'allow'
when we suppose
and some cherished archaisms
are correct Shakespearean.

Not to speak of the furled
consonants of lowlanders
shuttling obstinately
between bawn and mossland.

III

MacMorris, gallivanting
round the Globe, whinged
to courtier and groundling
who had heard tell of us

as going very bare
of learning, as wild hares,
as anatomies of death:
'What ish my nation?'

And sensibly, though so much
later, the wandering Bloom
replied, 'Ireland,' said Bloom,
'I was born here. Ireland.'

A NEW SONG

I met a girl from Derrygarve
And the name, a lost potent musk,
Recalled the river's long swerve,
A kingfisher's blue bolt at dusk

And stepping stones like black molars
Sunk in the ford, the shifty glaze
Of the whirlpool, the Moyola
Pleasuring beneath alder trees.

And Derrygarve, I thought, was just,
Vanished music, twilit water,
A smooth libation of the past
Poured by this chance vestal daughter.

But now our river tongues must rise
From licking deep in native haunts
To flood, with vowelling embrace,
Demesnes staked out in consonants.

And Castledawson we'll enlist
And Upperlands, each planted bawn—
Like bleaching-greens resumed by grass—
A vocable, as rath and bullaun.

THE OTHER SIDE

Thigh-deep in sedge and marigolds
a neighbour laid his shadow
on the stream, vouching

'It's poor as Lazarus, that ground,'
and brushed away
among the shaken leafage:

I lay where his lea sloped
to meet our fallow,
nested on moss and rushes,

my ear swallowing
his fabulous, biblical dismissal,
that tongue of chosen people.

When he would stand like that
on the other side, white-haired,
swinging his blackthorn

at the marsh weeds,
he prophesied above our scraggy acres,
then turned away

towards his promised furrows
on the hill, a wake of pollen
drifting to our bank, next season's tares.

II

For days we would rehearse
each patriarchal dictum:
Lazarus, the Pharaoh, Solomon

and David and Goliath rolled
magnificently, like loads of hay
too big for our small lanes,

or faltered on a rut—
'Your side of the house, I believe,
hardly rule by the book at all.'

His brain was a whitewashed kitchen
hung with texts, swept tidy
as the body o' the kirk.

III

Then sometimes when the rosary was dragging
mournfully on in the kitchen
we would hear his step round the gable

though not until after the litany
would the knock come to the door
and the casual whistle strike up

on the doorstep. 'A right-looking night,'
he might say, 'I was dandering by
and says I, I might as well call.'

But now I stand behind him
in the dark yard, in the moan of prayers.
He puts a hand in a pocket

or taps a little tune with the blackthorn
shyly, as if he were party to
lovemaking or a stranger's weeping.

Should I slip away, I wonder,
or go up and touch his shoulder
and talk about the weather

or the price of grass-seed?

from A NORTHERN HOARD

And some in dreams assured were
Of the Spirit that plagued us so

1. ROOTS

Leaf membranes lid the window.
In the streetlamp's glow
Your body's moonstruck
To drifted barrow, sunk glacial rock.

And all shifts dreamily as you keen
Far off, turning from the din
Of gunshot, siren and clucking gas
Out there beyond each curtained terrace

Where the fault is opening. The touch of love,
Your warmth heaving to the first move,
Grows helpless in our old Gomorrah.
We petrify or uproot now.

I'll dream it for us before dawn
When the pale sniper steps down
And I approach the shrub.
I've soaked by moonlight in tidal blood

A mandrake, lodged human fork,
Earth sac, limb of the dark;
And I wound its damp smelly loam
And stop my ears against the scream.

3. STUMP

I am riding to plague again.
Sometimes under a sooty wash
From the grate in the burnt-out gable
I see the needy in a small pow-wow.
What do I say if they wheel out their dead?
I'm cauterized, a black stump of home.

5. TINDER

We picked flints,
Pale and dirt-veined,

So small finger and thumb
Ached around them;

Cold beads of history and home
We fingered, a cave-mouth flame

Of leaf and stick
Trembling at the mind's wick.

We clicked stone on stone
That sparked a weak flame-pollen

And failed, our knuckle joints
Striking as often as the flints.

What did we know then
Of tinder, charred linen and iron,

Huddled at dusk in a ring,
Our fists shut, our hope shrunken?

What could strike a blaze
From our dead igneous days?

Now we squat on cold cinder,
Red-eyed, after the flames' soft thunder

And our thoughts settle like ash.
We face the tundra's whistling brush

With new history, flint and iron,
Cast-offs, scraps, nail, canine.

THE TOLLUND MAN

I

Some day I will go to Aarhus
To see his peat-brown head,
The mild pods of his eye-lids,
His pointed skin cap.

In the flat country nearby
Where they dug him out,
His last gruel of winter seeds
Caked in his stomach,

Naked except for
The cap, noose and girdle,
I will stand a long time.
Bridegroom to the goddess,

She tightened her torc on him
And opened her fen,
Those dark juices working
Him to a saint's kept body,

Trove of the turfcutters'
Honeycombed workings.
Now his stained face
Reposes at Aarhus.

I could risk blasphemy,
Consecrate the cauldron bog
Our holy ground and pray
Him to make germinate

The scattered, ambushed
Flesh of labourers,
Stockinged corpses
Laid out in the farmyards,

Tell-tale skin and teeth
Flecking the sleepers
Of four young brothers, trailed
For miles along the lines.

III

Something of his sad freedom
As he rode the tumbril
Should come to me, driving,
Saying the names

Tollund, Grauballe, Nebelgard,
Watching the pointing hands
Of country people,
Not knowing their tongue.

Out there in Jutland
In the old man-killing parishes
I will feel lost,
Unhappy and at home.

NERTHUS

For beauty, say an ash-fork staked in peat,
Its long grains gathering to the gouged split;

A seasoned, unsleeved taker of the weather,
Where kesh and loaning finger out to heather.

WEDDING DAY

I am afraid.
Sound has stopped in the day
And the images reel over
And over. Why all those tears,

The wild grief on his face
Outside the taxi? The sap
Of mourning rises
In our waving guests.

You sing behind the tall cake
Like a deserted bride
Who persists, demented,
And goes through the ritual.

When I went to the gents
There was a skewered heart
And a legend of love. Let me
Sleep on your breast to the airport.

SUMMER HOME

I

Was it wind off the dumps
or something in heat

dogging us, the summer gone sour,
a fouled nest incubating somewhere?

Whose fault, I wondered, inquisitor
of the possessed air.

To realize suddenly,
whip off the mat

that was larval, moving—
and scald, scald, scald.

II

Bushing the door, my arms full
of wild cherry and rhododendron,
I hear her small lost weeping
through the hall, that bells and hoarsens
on my name, my name.

O love, here is the blame.

The loosened flowers between us
gather in, compose
for a May altar of sorts.
These frank and falling blooms
soon taint to a sweet chrism.

Attend. Anoint the wound.

III

O we tented our wound all right
under the homely sheet

and lay as if the cold flat of a blade
had winded us.

More and more I postulate
thick healings, like now

as you bend in the shower
water lives down the tilting stoups of your breasts.

IV

With a final
unmusical drive
long grains begin
to open and split

ahead and once more
we sap
thc white, trodden
path to the heart.

My children weep out the hot foreign night.
We walk the floor, my foul mouth takes it out
On you and we lie stiff till dawn
Attends the pillow, and the maize, and vine

That holds its filling burden to the light.
Yesterday rocks sang when we tapped
Stalactites in the cave's old, dripping dark—
Our love calls tiny as a tuning fork.

SERENADES

The Irish nightingale
Is a sedge-warbler,
A little bird with a big voice
Kicking up a racket all night.

Not what you'd expect
From the musical nation.
I haven't even heard one—
Nor an owl, for that matter.

My serenades have been
The broken voice of a crow
In a draught or a dream,
The wheeze of bats

Or the ack-ack
Of the tramp corncrake
Lost in a no man's land
Between combines and chemicals.

So fill the bottles, love,
Leave them inside their cots.
And if they do wake us, well,
So would the sedge-warbler.

SHORE WOMAN

Man to the hills, woman to the shore.
                                    Gaelic proverb

I have crossed the dunes with their whistling bent
Where dry loose sand was riddling round the air
And I'm walking the firm margin. White pocks
Of cockle, blanched roofs of clam and oyster
Hoard the moonlight, woven and unwoven
Off the bay. At the far rocks
A pale sud comes and goes.

Under boards the mackerel slapped to death
Yet still we took them in at every cast,
Stiff flails of cold convulsed with their first breath.
My line plumbed certainly the undertow,
Loaded against me once I went to draw
And flashed and fattened up towards the light.
He was all business in the stern. I called
'This is so easy that it's hardly right,'
But he unhooked and coped with frantic fish
Without speaking. Then suddenly it lulled,
We'd crossed where they were running, the line rose
Like a let-down and I was conscious
How far we'd drifted out beyond the head.
'Count them up at your end,' was all he said
Before I saw the porpoises' thick backs
Cartwheeling like the flywheels of the tide,
Soapy and shining. To have seen a hill

Splitting the water could not have numbed me more
Than the close irruption of that school,
Tight viscous muscle, hooped from tail to snout,
Each one revealed complete as it bowled out
And under.
                    They will attack a boat.
I knew it and I asked him to put in
But he would not, declared it was a yarn
My people had been fooled by far too long
And he would prove it now and settle it.
Maybe he shrank when those sloped oily backs
Propelled towards us: I lay and screamed
Under splashed brine in an open rocking boat
Feeling each dunt and slither through the timber,
Sick at their huge pleasures in the water.

I sometimes walk this strand for thanksgiving
Or maybe it's to get away from him
Skittering his spit across the stove. Here
Is the taste of safety, the shelving sand
Harbours no worse than razor-shell or crab—
Though my father recalls carcasses of whales
Collapsed and gasping, right up to the dunes.
But to-night such moving sinewed dreams lie out
In darker fathoms, far beyond the head.
Astray upon a debris of scrubbed shells
Between parched dunes and salivating wave,
I have rights on this fallow avenue,
A membrane between moonlight and my shadow.

MAIGHDEAN MARA

For Seán O h-Eochaidh

I

She sleeps now, her cold breasts
Dandled by undertow,
Her hair lifted and laid.
Undulant slow seawracks
Cast about shin and thigh,
Bangles of wort, drifting
Weeds catch, dislodge gently.

This is the great first sleep
Of homecoming, eight
Land years between hearth and
Bed steeped and dishevelled.
Her magic garment al-
most ocean-tinctured still.

II

He stole her garment as
She combed her hair: follow
Was all that she could do.
He hid it in the eaves
And charmed her there, four walls,
Warm floor, man-love nightly
In earshot of the waves.

She suffered milk and birth—
She had no choice—conjured
Patterns of home and drained
The tidesong from her voice.
Then the thatcher came and stuck
Her garment in a stack.
Children carried tales back.

III

In night air, entering
Foam, she wrapped herself
With smoke-reeks from his thatch,
Straw-musts and films of mildew.
She dipped his secret there
Forever and uncharmed

Accents of fisher wives,
The dead hold of bedrooms,
Dread of the night and morrow,
Her children's brush and combs.
She sleeps now, her cold breasts
Dandled by undertow.

LIMBO

Fishermen at Ballyshannon
Netted an infant last night
Along with the salmon.
An illegitimate spawning,

A small one thrown back
To the waters. But I'm sure
As she stood in the shallows
Ducking him tenderly

Till the frozen knobs of her wrists
Were dead as the gravel,
He was a minnow with hooks
Tearing her open.

She waded in under
The sign of her cross.
He was hauled in with the fish.
Now limbo will be

A cold glitter of souls
Through some far briny zone.
Even Christ's palms, unhealed,
Smart and cannot fish there.

BYE-CHILD

He was discovered in the henhouse
where she had confined him. He was
incapable of saying anything.

When the lamp glowed,
A yolk of light
In their back window,
The child in the outhouse
Put his eye to a chink—

Little henhouse boy,
Sharp-faced as new moons
Remembered, your photo still
Glimpsed like a rodent
On the floor of my mind,

Little moon man,
Kennelled and faithful
At the foot of the yard,
Your frail shape, luminous,
Weightless, is stirring the dust,

The cobwebs, old droppings
Under the roosts
And dry smells from scraps
She put through your trapdoor
Morning and evening.

After those footsteps, silence;
Vigils, solitudes, fasts,

Unchristened tears,
A puzzled love of the light.
But now you speak at last

With a remote mime
Of something beyond patience,
Your gaping wordless proof
Of lunar distances
Travelled beyond love.

GOOD-NIGHT

A latch lifting, an edged den of light
Opens across the yard. Out of the low door
They stoop into the honeyed corridor,
Then walk straight through the wall of the dark.

A puddle, cobble-stones, jambs and doorstep
Are set steady in a block of brightness.
Till she strides in again beyond her shadows
And cancels everything behind her.

WESTERING

In California

I sit under Rand McNally's
'Official Map of the Moon'—
The colour of frogskin,
Its enlarged pores held

Open and one called
'Pitiscus' at eye level—
Recalling the last night
In Donegal, my shadow

Neat upon the whitewash
From her bony shine,
The cobbles of the yard
Lit pale as eggs.

Summer had been a free fall
Ending there,
The empty amphitheatre
Of the west. Good Friday

We had started out
Past shopblinds drawn on the afternoon,
Cars stilled outside still churches,
Bikes tilting to a wall;

We drove by,
A dwindling interruption
As clappers smacked
On a bare altar

And congregations bent
To the studded crucifix.
What nails dropped out that hour?
Roads unreeled, unreeled

Falling light as casts
Laid down
On shining waters.
Under the moon's stigmata

Six thousand miles away,
I imagine untroubled dust,
A loosening gravity,
Christ weighing by his hands.

from
North

MOSSBAWN: TWO POEMS IN DEDICATION

For Mary Heaney

1. SUNLIGHT

There was a sunlit absence.
The helmeted pump in the yard
heated its iron,
water honeyed

in the slung bucket
and the sun stood
like a griddle cooling
against the wall

of each long afternoon.
So, her hands scuffled
over the bakeboard,
the reddening stove

sent its plaque of heat
against her where she stood
in a floury apron
by the window.

Now she dusts the board
with a goose's wing,
now sits, broad-lapped,
with whitened nails

and measling shins:
here is a space
again, the scone rising
to the tick of two clocks.

And here is love
like a tinsmith's scoop
sunk past its gleam
in the meal-bin.

2. THE SEED CUTTERS

They seem hundreds of years away. Breughel,
You'll know them if I can get them true.
They kneel under the hedge in a half-circle
Behind a windbreak wind is breaking through.
They are the seed cutters. The tuck and frill
Of leaf-sprout is on the seed potatoes
Buried under that straw. With time to kill
They are taking their time. Each sharp knife goes
Lazily halving each root that falls apart
In the palm of the hand: a milky gleam,
And, at the centre, a dark watermark.
O calendar customs! Under the broom
Yellowing over them, compose the frieze
With all of us there, our anonymities.

FUNERAL RITES

I

I shouldered a kind of manhood
stepping in to lift the coffins
of dead relations.
They had been laid out

in tainted rooms,
their eyelids glistening,
their dough-white hands
shackled in rosary beads.

Their puffed knuckles
had unwrinkled, the nails
were darkened, the wrists
obediently sloped.

The dulse-brown shroud,
the quilted satin cribs:
I knelt courteously
admiring it all

as wax melted down
and veined the candles,
the flames hovering
to the women hovering

behind me.
And always, in a corner,
the coffin lid,
its nail-heads dressed

with little gleaming crosses.
Dear soapstone masks,
kissing their igloo brows
had to suffice

before the nails were sunk
and the black glacier
of each funeral
pushed away.

II

Now as news comes in
of each neighbourly murder
we pine for ceremony,
customary rhythms:

the temperate footsteps
of a cortège, winding past
each blinded home.
I would restore

the great chambers of Boyne,
prepare a sepulchre
under the cupmarked stones.
Out of side-streets and bye-roads

purring family cars
nose into line,

the whole country tunes
to the muffled drumming

of ten thousand engines.
Somnambulant women,
left behind, move
through emptied kitchens

imagining our slow triumph
towards the mounds.
Quiet as a serpent
in its grassy boulevard

the procession drags its tail
out of the Gap of the North
as its head already enters
the megalithic doorway.

III

When they have put the stone
back in its mouth
we will drive north again
past Strang and Carling fjords

the cud of memory
allayed for once, arbitration
of the feud placated,
imagining those under the hill

disposed like Gunnar
who lay beautiful
inside his burial mound,
though dead by violence

and unavenged.
Men said that he was chanting
verses about honour
and that four lights burned

in corners of the chamber:
which opened then, as he turned
with a joyful face
to look at the moon.

NORTH

I returned to a long strand,
the hammered shod of a bay,
and found only the secular
powers of the Atlantic thundering.

I faced the unmagical
invitations of Iceland,
the pathetic colonies
of Greenland, and suddenly

those fabulous raiders,
those lying in Orkney and Dublin
measured against
their long swords rusting,

those in the solid
belly of stone ships,
those hacked and glinting
in the gravel of thawed streams

were ocean-deafened voices
warning me, lifted again
in violence and epiphany.
The longship's swimming tongue

was buoyant with hindsight—
it said Thor's hammer swung
to geography and trade,
thick-witted couplings and revenges,

the hatreds and behindbacks
of the althing, lies and women,
exhaustions nominated peace,
memory incubating the spilled blood.

It said, 'Lie down
in the word-hoard, burrow
the coil and gleam
of your furrowed brain.

Compose in darkness.
Expect aurora borealis
in the long foray
but no cascade of light.

Keep your eye clear
as the bleb of the icicle,
trust the feel of what nubbed treasure
your hands have known.'

VIKING DUBLIN:
TRIAL PIECES

I

It could be a jaw-bone
or a rib or a portion cut
from something sturdier:
anyhow, a small outline

was incised, a cage
or trellis to conjure in.
Like a child's tongue
following the toils

of his calligraphy,
like an eel swallowed
in a basket of eels,
the line amazes itself

eluding the hand
that fed it,
a bill in flight,
a swimming nostril.

II

These are trial pieces,
the craft's mystery

improvised on bone:
foliage, bestiaries,

interlacings elaborate
as the netted routes
of ancestry and trade.
That have to be

magnified on display
so that the nostril
is a migrant prow
sniffing the Liffey,

swanning it up to the ford,
dissembling itself
in antler combs, bone pins,
coins, weights, scale-pans.

III

Like a long sword
sheathed in its moisting
burial clays,
the keel stuck fast

in the slip of the bank,
its clinker-built hull
spined and plosive
as *Dublin*.

And now we reach in
for shards of the vertebrae,
the ribs of hurdle,
the mother-wet caches—

and for this trial piece
incised by a child,
a longship, a buoyant
migrant line.

IV

That enters my longhand,
turns cursive, unscarfing
a zoomorphic wake,
a worm of thought

I follow into the mud.
I am Hamlet the Dane,
skull-handler, parablist,
smeller of rot

in the state, infused
with its poisons,
pinioned by ghosts
and affections,

murders and pieties,
coming to consciousness
by jumping in graves,
dithering, blathering.

V

Come fly with me,
come sniff the wind
with the expertise
of the Vikings—

neighbourly, scoretaking
killers, haggers

and hagglers, gombeen-men,
hoarders of grudges and gain.

With a butcher's aplomb
they spread out your lungs
and made you warm wings
for your shoulders.

Old fathers, be with us.
Old cunning assessors
of feuds and of sites
for ambush or town.

VI

'Did you ever hear tell,'
said Jimmy Farrell,
'of the skulls they have
in the city of Dublin?

White skulls and black skulls
and yellow skulls, and some
with full teeth, and some
haven't only but one,'

and compounded history
in the pan of 'an old Dane,
maybe, was drowned
in the Flood.'

My words lick around
cobbled quays, go hunting
lightly as pampooties
over the skull-capped ground.

BOG QUEEN

I lay waiting
between turf-face and demesne wall,
between heathery levels
and glass-toothed stone.

My body was braille
for the creeping influences:
dawn suns groped over my head
and cooled at my feet,

through my fabrics and skins
the seeps of winter
digested me,
the illiterate roots

pondered and died
in the cavings
of stomach and socket.
I lay waiting

on the gravel bottom,
my brain darkening,
a jar of spawn
fermenting underground

dreams of Baltic amber.
Bruised berries under my nails,
the vital hoard reducing
in the crock of the pelvis.

My diadem grew carious,
gemstones dropped
in the peat floe
like the bearings of history.

My sash was a black glacier
wrinkling, dyed weaves
and phoenician stitchwork
retted on my breasts'

soft moraines.
I knew winter cold
like the nuzzle of fjords
at my thighs—

the soaked fledge, the heavy
swaddle of hides.
My skull hibernated
in the wet nest of my hair.

Which they robbed.
I was barbered
and stripped
by a turfcutter's spade

who veiled me again
and packed coomb softly
between the stone jambs
at my head and my feet.

Till a peer's wife bribed him.
The plait of my hair,
a slimy birth-cord
of bog, had been cut

and I rose from the dark,
hacked bone, skull-ware,
frayed stitches, tufts,
small gleams on the bank.

THE GRAUBALLE MAN

As if he had been poured
in tar, he lies
on a pillow of turf
and seems to weep

the black river of himself.
The grain of his wrists
is like bog oak,
the ball of his heel

like a basalt egg.
His instep has shrunk
cold as a swan's foot
or a wet swamp root.

His hips are the ridge
and purse of a mussel,
his spine an eel arrested
under a glisten of mud.

The head lifts,
the chin is a visor
raised above the vent
of his slashed throat

that has tanned and toughened.
The cured wound
opens inwards to a dark
elderberry place.

Who will say 'corpse'
to his vivid cast?
Who will say 'body'
to his opaque repose?

And his rusted hair,
a mat unlikely
as a foetus's.
I first saw his twisted face

in a photograph,
a head and shoulder
out of the peat,
bruised like a forceps baby,

but now he lies
perfected in my memory,
down to the red horn
of his nails,

hung in the scales
with beauty and atrocity:
with the Dying Gaul
too strictly compassed

on his shield,
with the actual weight
of each hooded victim,
slashed and dumped.

PUNISHMENT

I can feel the tug
of the halter at the nape
of her neck, the wind
on her naked front.

It blows her nipples
to amber beads,
it shakes the frail rigging
of her ribs.

I can see her drowned
body in the bog,
the weighing stone,
the floating rods and boughs.

Under which at first
she was a barked sapling
that is dug up
oak-bone, brain-firkin:

her shaved head
like a stubble of black corn,
her blindfold a soiled bandage,
her noose a ring

to store
the memories of love.
Little adulteress,
before they punished you

you were flaxen-haired,
undernourished, and your
tar-black face was beautiful.
My poor scapegoat,

I almost love you
but would have cast, I know,
the stones of silence.
I am the artful voyeur

of your brain's exposed
and darkened combs,
your muscles' webbing
and all your numbered bones:

I who have stood dumb
when your betraying sisters,
cauled in tar,
wept by the railings,

who would connive
in civilized outrage
yet understand the exact
and tribal, intimate revenge.

STRANGE FRUIT

Here is the girl's head like an exhumed gourd.
Oval-faced, prune-skinned, prune-stones for teeth.
They unswaddled the wet fern of her hair
And made an exhibition of its coil,
Let the air at her leathery beauty.
Pash of tallow, perishable treasure:
Her broken nose is dark as a turf clod,
Her eyeholes blank as pools in the old workings.
Diodorus Siculus confessed
His gradual ease among the likes of this:
Murdered, forgotten, nameless, terrible
Beheaded girl, outstaring axe
And beatification, outstaring
What had begun to feel like reverence.

KINSHIP

I

Kinned by hieroglyphic
peat on a spreadfield
to the strangled victim,
the love-nest in the bracken,

I step through origins
like a dog turning
its memories of wilderness
on the kitchen mat:

the bog floor shakes,
water cheeps and lisps
as I walk down
rushes and heather.

I love this turf-face,
its black incisions,
the cooped secrets
of process and ritual;

I love the spring
off the ground,
each bank a gallows drop,
each open pool

the unstopped mouth
of an urn, a moon-drinker,
not to be sounded
by the naked eye.

II

Quagmire, swampland, morass:
the slime kingdoms,
domains of the cold-blooded,
of mud pads and dirtied eggs.

But *bog*
meaning soft,
the fall of windless rain,
pupil of amber.

Ruminant ground,
digestion of mollusc
and seed-pod,
deep pollen bin.

Earth-pantry, bone-vault,
sun-bank, enbalmer
of votive goods
and sabred fugitives.

Insatiable bride.
Sword-swallower,
casket, midden,
floe of history.

Ground that will strip
its dark side,

nesting ground,
outback of my mind.

III

I found a turf-spade
hidden under bracken,
laid flat, and overgrown
with a green fog.

As I raised it
the soft lips of the growth
muttered and split,
a tawny rut

opening at my feet
like a shed skin,
the shaft wettish
as I sank it upright

and beginning to
steam in the sun.
And now they have twinned
that obelisk:

among the stones,
under a bearded cairn
a love-nest is disturbed,
catkin and bog-cotton tremble

as they raise up
the cloven oak-limb.
I stand at the edge of centuries
facing a goddess.

IV

This centre holds
and spreads,
sump and seedbed,
a bag of waters

and a melting grave.
The mothers of autumn
sour and sink,
ferments of husk and leaf

deepen their ochres.
Mosses come to a head,
heather unseeds,
brackens deposit

their bronze.
This is the vowel of earth
dreaming its root
in flowers and snow,

mutation of weathers
and seasons,
a windfall composing
the floor it rots into.

I grew out of all this
like a weeping willow
inclined to
the appetites of gravity.

V

The hand carved felloes
of the turf-cart wheels
buried in a litter
of turf mould,

the cupid's bow
of the tail-board,
the socketed lips
of the cribs:

I deified the man
who rode there,
god of the waggon,
the hearth-feeder.

I was his privileged
attendant, a bearer
of bread and drink,
the squire of his circuits.

When summer died
and wives forsook the fields
we were abroad,
saluted, given right-of-way.

Watch our progress
down the haw-lit hedges,
my manly pride
when he speaks to me.

And you, Tacitus,
observe how I make my grove
on an old crannog
piled by the fearful dead:

a desolate peace.
Our mother ground
is sour with the blood
of her faithful,

they lie gargling
in her sacred heart
as the legions stare
from the ramparts.

Come back to this
'island of the ocean'
where nothing will suffice.
Read the inhumed faces

of casualty and victim;
report us fairly,
how we slaughter
for the common good

and shave the heads
of the notorious,
how the goddess swallows
our love and terror.

ACT OF UNION

I

To-night, a first movement, a pulse,
As if the rain in bogland gathered head
To slip and flood: a bog-burst,
A gash breaking open the ferny bed.
Your back is a firm line of eastern coast
And arms and legs are thrown
Beyond your gradual hills. I caress
The heaving province where our past has grown.
I am the tall kingdom over your shoulder
That you would neither cajole nor ignore.
Conquest is a lie. I grow older
Conceding your half-independent shore
Within whose borders now my legacy
Culminates inexorably.

II

And I am still imperially
Male, leaving you with the pain,
The rending process in the colony,
The battering ram, the boom burst from within.
The act sprouted an obstinate fifth column
Whose stance is growing unilateral.

His heart beneath your heart is a wardrum
Mustering force. His parasitical
And ignorant little fists already
Beat at your borders and I know they're cocked
At me across the water. No treaty
I foresee will salve completely your tracked
And stretchmarked body, the big pain
That leaves you raw, like opened ground, again.

HERCULES AND ANTAEUS

Sky-born and royal,
snake-choker, dung-heaver,
his mind big with golden apples,
his future hung with trophies,

Hercules has the measure
of resistance and black powers
feeding off the territory.
Antaeus, the mould-hugger,

is weaned at last:
a fall was a renewal
but now he is raised up—
the challenger's intelligence

is a spur of light,
a blue prong graiping him
out of his element
into a dream of loss

and origins—the cradling dark,
the river-veins, the secret gullies
of his strength,
the hatching grounds

of cave and souterrain,
he has bequeathed it all
to elegists. Balor will die
and Byrthnoth and Sitting Bull.

Hercules lifts his arms
in a remorseless V,
his triumph unassailed
by the powers he has shaken

and lifts and banks Antaeus
high as a profiled ridge,
a sleeping giant,
pap for the dispossessed.

from SINGING SCHOOL

1. THE MINISTRY OF FEAR
For Seamus Deane

Well, as Kavanagh said, we have lived
In important places. The lonely scarp
Of St Columb's College, where I billeted
For six years, overlooked your Bogside.
I gazed into new worlds: the inflamed throat
Of Brandywell, its floodlit dogtrack,
The throttle of the hare. In the first week
I was so homesick I couldn't even eat
The biscuits left to sweeten my exile.
I threw them over the fence one night
In September 1951
When the lights of houses in the Lecky Road
Were amber in the fog. It was an act
Of stealth.
              Then Belfast, and then Berkeley.
Here's two on's are sophisticated,
Dabbling in verses till they have become
A life: from bulky envelopes arriving
In vacation time to slim volumes
Despatched 'with the author's compliments'.
Those poems in longhand, ripped from the wire spine
Of your exercise book, bewildered me—
Vowels and ideas bandied free
As the seed-pods blowing off our sycamores.
I tried to write about the sycamores

And innovated a South Derry rhyme
With *hushed* and *lulled* full chimes for *pushed* and *pulled*.
Those hobnailed boots from beyond the mountain
Were walking, by God, all over the fine
Lawns of elocution.

                    Have our accents
Changed? 'Catholics, in general, don't speak
As well as students from the Protestant schools.'
Remember that stuff? Inferiority
Complexes, stuff that dreams were made on.
'What's your name, Heaney?'

                             'Heaney, Father.'

                                   'Fair
Enough.'
        On my first day, the leather strap
Went epileptic in the Big Study,
Its echoes plashing over our bowed heads,
But I still wrote home that a boarder's life
Was not so bad, shying as usual.

On long vacations, then, I came to life
In the kissing seat of an Austin Sixteen
Parked at a gable, the engine running,
My fingers tight as ivy on her shoulders,
A light left burning for her in the kitchen.
And heading back for home, the summer's
Freedom dwindling night by night, the air
All moonlight and a scent of hay, policemen
Swung their crimson flashlamps, crowding round
The car like black cattle, snuffing and pointing
The muzzle of a sten-gun in my eye:
'What's your name, driver?'

                       'Seamus . . .'

                          Seamus?

They once read my letters at a roadblock
And shone their torches on your hieroglyphics,
'Svelte dictions' in a very florid hand.

Ulster was British, but with no rights on
The English lyric: all around us, though
We hadn't named it, the ministry of fear.

His bicycle stood at the window-sill,
The rubber cowl of a mud-splasher
Skirting the front mudguard,
Its fat black handlegrips

Heating in sunlight, the 'spud'
Of the dynamo gleaming and cocked back,
The pedal treads hanging relieved
Of the boot of the law.

His cap was upside down
On the floor, next his chair.
The line of its pressure ran like a bevel
In his slightly sweating hair.

He had unstrapped
The heavy ledger, and my father
Was making tillage returns
In acres, roods, and perches.

Arithmetic and fear.
I sat staring at the polished holster
With its buttoned flap, the braid cord
Looped into the revolver butt.

'Any other root crops?
Mangolds? Marrowstems? Anything like that?'
'No.' But was there not a line
Of turnips where the seed ran out

In the potato field? I assumed
Small guilts and sat
Imagining the black hole in the barracks.
He stood up, shifted the baton-case

Further round on his belt,
Closed the domesday book,
Fitted his cap back with two hands,
And looked at me as he said goodbye.

A shadow bobbed in the window.
He was snapping the carrier spring
Over the ledger. His boot pushed off
And the bicycle ticked, ticked, ticked.

5. FOSTERAGE

For Michael McLaverty

'Description is revelation!' Royal
Avenue, Belfast, 1962,
A Saturday afternoon, glad to meet
Me, newly cubbed in language, he gripped
My elbow. 'Listen. Go your own way.
Do your own work. Remember
Katherine Mansfield—*I will tell*
How the laundry basket squeaked . . . that note of exile.'
But to hell with overstating it:
'Don't have the veins bulging in your biro.'
And then, 'Poor Hopkins!' I have the *Journals*
He gave me, underlined, his buckled self
Obeisant to their pain. He discerned
The lineaments of patience everywhere
And fostered me and sent me out, with words
Imposing on my tongue like obols.

6. EXPOSURE

It is December in Wicklow:
Alders dripping, birches
Inheriting the last light,
The ash tree cold to look at.

A comet that was lost
Should be visible at sunset,
Those million tons of light
Like a glimmer of haws and rose-hips,

And I sometimes see a falling star.
If I could come on meteorite!
Instead I walk through damp leaves,
Husks, the spent flukes of autumn,

Imagining a hero
On some muddy compound,
His gift like a slingstone
Whirled for the desperate.

How did I end up like this?
I often think of my friends'
Beautiful prismatic counselling
And the anvil brains of some who hate me

As I sit weighing and weighing
My responsible *tristia*.
For what? For the ear? For the people?
For what is said behind-backs?

Rain comes down through the alders,
Its low conducive voices
Mutter about let-downs and erosions
And yet each drop recalls

The diamond absolutes.
I am neither internee nor informer;
An inner émigré, grown long-haired
And thoughtful; a wood-kerne

Escaped from the massacre,
Taking protective colouring
From bole and bark, feeling
Every wind that blows;

Who, blowing up these sparks
For their meagre heat, have missed
The once-in-a-lifetime portent,
The comet's pulsing rose.